❖ The Boy ❖
Who Cried Wolf

TONY ROSS

Dial Books for Young Readers

New York

For Zöe and Katy

Published in the United States 1985 by
Dial Books for Young Readers
A Division of E. P. Dutton, Inc.
2 Park Avenue
New York, New York 10016
First published in Great Britain by Andersen Press
Copyright © 1985 by Tony Ross
Printed in Italy
Design by Susan Lu
First Edition
US
10 9 8 7 6 5 4 3 2 1

Library of Congress Cataloging in Publication Data
Ross, Tony. The boy who cried wolf.
Summary: In this contemporary retelling of a
traditional tale Willy cries "wolf" to get out of ordeals,
like taking a bath or going to his violin lesson,
until the wolf really appears.
1. Children's stories, American.
[1. Behavior—Fiction. 2. Wolves—Fiction.] I. Title.
PZ7.R71992Bo 1985   [E]   84-23273
ISBN 0-8037-0193-4

The art for each picture consists of a black ink
and watercolor painting, which is camera-separated
and reproduced in full color.

Once upon a time a little boy lived on this side
of the mountains. His name was Willy.

On the other side of the mountains a wolf lived
in the lap of luxury. Nobody ever asked *his* name.

The wolf had fine manners (for a wolf).
Sometimes he put on his dinner jacket...

and came over the mountains
...for dinner.

Because the wolf liked dining on people, everybody on this side of the mountains was afraid of him. So...

whenever Willy had to do something he didn't
want to, like take a bath,

he would cry "wolf" (even if the wolf was nowhere to be seen).
Because everybody was afraid of the wolf...

Willy was left alone to do just what he wanted.

Once a week Willy went for his violin lesson.
Because he hated his lessons...

he cried "wolf," even though the wolf was not around.

Then Willy was left alone to play the kind of music
he liked.

Sometimes Willy even cried "wolf"
just for the fun of it.

One day Willy was riding in the mountains
when the wolf jumped out from the rocks.

"WOLF!" cried Willy.
He ran back to town crying "WOLF, WOLF"
all the way.

"WOLF!" cried Willy, but his grandmother didn't believe him. Willy always cried "wolf."
"Tell me another one!" she said.

"WOLF" cried Willy, but nobody listened.

"Save me from the WOLF!" shrieked Willy,
but everybody laughed.
"Willy's crying 'wolf' again," they said.

At last the wolf caught up with Willy.
"You shouldn't have told so many lies!" said
the grown-ups sternly.

The wolf heard the grown-ups and changed his mind about eating Willy.

He ate the grown-ups instead.

Then...

he changed his mind again and had Willy for dessert.

C'est la vie.